CORNELL DYER AND THE "MISTICAL" BEING

An Adventures of Cornell Dyer
supernatural mystery

Denise M. Baran-Unland

In collaboration with Rebekah Baran

Illustrated by Sue Midlock

This book is lovingly dedicated to the reader, whoever you might be.

"What arrested me on the spot – and with a shock much greater than any vision had allowed for – was the sense that my imagination had, in a flash, turned real. He did stand there!"

— **Henry James, Turn of the Screw**

CONTENTS

PROLOGUE

"March! March! March! March! March!"

It had been a long time since Dagobert had shouted those words to his soldiers.

In fact, it had been a long time since Dagobert had commanded soldiers at all.

Dagobert and his fellow officers were part of the thirty thousand German soldiers that the British Army had hired to help fight during the Revolutionary War.

And Dagobert and his fellow officers were also part of the nine hundred soldiers that General George Washington and the Continental Army had captured after the Battle of Trenton on December 26, 1776.

Don't get him wrong. The soldiers were treated well. But it was better to be an officer.

"Kristoph," Dagobert said to his sleeping companion in the coach. "Aren't you excited?"

"Ja," Kristoph mumbled.

The officers had ridden in this train of carriages for days. They crossed into Virginia just after dark. Soon, they would be free. Dagobert could not wait.

The carriages stopped. This was it.

"Everybody out!" someone roared.

"Let's go Kristoph." Dagobert poked his friend. "Wake up! It is time!"

They opened door and stepped out.

SPLASH!

Water sloshed up to their waists.

"Hey!" the officers cried, panicked, as they struggled to get out of the muck that held them fast. "Hey! Help us!"

"FIRE!"

Then the shots rang out, and the cries for help stopped.

CHAPTER ONE: LOST AT THE LAKE

"Humph!" Cornell exclaimed. "What kind of town can't get its name right?

The gas station attendant pushed up his thick glasses with a shaking finger. He smoothed his graying black hair with a trembling hand.

The sun squeezed through the dirty windowpanes. The sun glinted off the dusty metal nametag on the pocket of the attendant's blue collared shirt.

The name tag read: Kirk Winkler.

"Si..si...sir," Kirk stammered in voice that had a faint German accent. "I..I...can't explain it. The town's name has changed almost daily since I was a boy." He held out his hand. "May I?"

"Humph," Cornell said again.

But he set the wrinkled road map on the counter.

Kirk traced a curving line with that same shaking finger.

"See? If you just take this road south of Virginia for the next three hours, you will arrive at..."

"At what?" Cornell demanded.

"I...I can't pronounce it," Kirk confessed. "But if you follow this road, you will arrive at the town. Business or pleasure?"

"Business," Cornell said. "I am the great supernatural super sleuth Cornell Dyer. I specialize in Amulets, Fortune-Telling (with and without cards), Ghost-Hunting, Horoscopes, Numerology, Palm-Reading, Potions, Séances, Spells, Vampire-Slaying, controlling zombie populations, and deactivating Moravian pink goblins and cold whispers."

"Ah," Kirk said with a gleam in his coal black eyes. "You will certainly find plenty of supernatural mysteries there." He refolded the map and gave it back to Cornell. "May I help you with anything else?"

"Yes," Cornell said. "I'll have six bottles of icy orange drink and three big bags of extra salty potato chips."

Ten minutes later, Cornell was behind the wheel in his giant motor home and zooming down the road Kirk had pointed out.

As Cornell drove, he replayed a certain phone call in his mind.

"Professor Dyer!" the woman scolded him. "When are you getting rid of the haunted lake in my back yard!"

"I'll be right there," Cornell said. "Just as soon as I have lunch and cross a few state lines."

Of course, Cornell was in no hurry to reach the town of...of...of...whatever it was called. Because along the way, other paying customers hired him, too.

So naturally Cornell had stopped to read palms, conduct a few séances, and whip up several dozen love potions.

Three hours later, Cornell was starving. He saw a sign for Hal's Drive-In Restaurant. So Cornell turned off the highway.

At Hal's Cornell ordered three hamburgers, two large hand-cut fries, and a super large homemade frosty root beer. He studied the map as he munched and slurped. Two hours to go until he arrived...there.

"All done?" the red-haired carhop in the white shirt and black tie asked, reaching for the plastic tray. Her green eyes glinted in the sunlight.

"Yep." Cornell folded the map and turned the key.

Two more hours later, Cornell veered off the main remote road and onto an even more remote road. He drove for ten more miles and then came to the end of the road. And at the end of this road was a house. He braked and put the motor home into park.

The house looked like a flat box with an overhanging flat roof.

Along with a sagging porch, the house had two large square windows and an old door between them. To Cornell, they looked like two eyes and a long nose.

In fact, Cornell felt the house was actually staring at him. That may sound strange to many people. But it did not sound strange to a supernatural super sleuth like Cornell Dyer.

Ghoul Garage in Nebraska had not only watched Cornell, it had followed him and spied on him, too.

The Castle of Creepy Cocoons didn't give Cornell didn't a moment of privacy until Cornell shut down its other-worldly computer network that hacked into people's thoughts.

So the notion of a house in the middle of nowhere at the end of a very remote road did not surprise Cornell.

But it might add another layer of mystery to solve.

A tall tree stood on each side of the house. And that was it.

It was just the house and two trees in the middle of a yellow-brown field.

Cornell switched the key to "off."

Well, he thought, time to find the lake.

He grabbed his get-rid-of-ghosts-in-lakes briefcase and opened the motor home door. Supernatural super sleuths are always prepared to vanquish ghosts from lakes, even when finding the lake was part of the mystery.

He thumped up the wooden steps and ran his hand though his greasy, curly black hair since he never carried a comb on him. Saturday was bath night. Today was only Monday.

Then Cornell raised his fist and banged on the screen door. That action also raised his purple T-shirt, so he tugged that politely into place. That reminded Cornell of something else: Cornell was out of clean clothes, too.

He was wearing his last pair of faded blue jeans and his last clean T-shirt. This shirt had the word BOO! stamped on it. But Cornell wasn't too worried. Laundry was part of his payment.

He raised his fist and banged again, harder this time. After twenty minutes and nine more knocks, the door slowly opened. A sullen teenager, black hair slicked back, glowered at him.

"You're him?" the teenager asked. He had ketchup stains on his white T-shirt.

"Young man, I am the great supernatural super sleuth Cornell Dyer. I specialize in Amulets, Fortune-Telling (with and without cards), Ghost-Hunting, Horoscopes, Numerology, Palm-Reading, Potions, Séances..."

"Yep. You're him. Grandmother is expecting you. Let's go."

The teenager led Cornell through a dingy hallway to a small living room that smelled of mildew and made a steady creak, creak, creak sound. The room was jammed full of scratched, broken, and dusty furniture, more furniture than a dozen antique furniture stores.

An old, old, old, old woman with dyed red hair and green eyes was rocking back and forth in one of the chairs with the energy of a small child.

"Cornell Dyer," the woman croaked in a loud, strong voice.

"Professor Cornell Dyer," Cornell corrected her.

She smiled. "Yes. Professor. I am Rosemary Müller. And this…"

Rosemary looked at the teen slouching against the door jamb. "This is my grandson. His name is Kenneth Tyler Müller."

"Ty," the teen corrected Rosemary. "I've told you to stop calling me…"

"Please, Professor," Rosemary gestured. "Have a seat."

Cornell looked around the room for an item that could hold his weight. He finally decided on a heavy coffee table. But he kept a grip on his briefcase.

"Where is the lake?" Cornell asked. "I'm here to get rid of the ghost."

Rosemary stopped rocking. "It's not that simple."

Cornell held up his briefcase. "Yes, it is. I have everything I need right here. Where is the lake?"

"You can't just get rid of the ghost, you see."

"Yes, I can."

Rosemary sighed. "Professor, ghosts have haunted our town ever since the Revolutionary War. 'They' say part of our town was built on buried soldiers that...died here."

"Well, that's an interesting tale," Cornell said as he rose. "I can get rid of those ghosts, too. Who can show me that part of town?"

"Kenneth...I mean Ty...could," Rosemary said. "I can't walk that far."

"We can take my motor home," Cornell said.

"No, you can't," Rosemary argued. "Ty?"

So Ty grabbed his leather jacket and headed for the door. Cornell grabbed his colorful patchwork blazer from his motor home and dropped the get-rid-of-ghosts-in-lakes briefcase near the door. Then he grabbed his all-purpose ghost-be-gone magical wand, which was hiding under the couch.

Cornell didn't know if he would see any ghosts. But he wanted to bring it – just in case.

Then Cornell locked his motor home and

pocketed the keys.

"I'm ready," Cornell said.

Ty scowled and plodded across the field. So that's why Cornell could not take the motor home. The field had no road. So Cornell had no place to drive the motor home.

Well, Cornell thought. One mystery solved.

They walked so long that Cornell wished he had brought a couple bottles of cold orange drink. Every few minutes, Cornell swatted a mosquito or two and waved away clouds of gnats.

After a long, long, long while, Cornell and Ty arrived at the edge of a hill overlooking a ghost town. Cornell knew it was a ghost town because he had watched lots of movies about ghost towns and their ramshackle buildings. And this town looked just like those movies.

Ty pointed. "That's it."

"So let's go," Cornell said.

Ty shook his head. "You'd have to be brainless go any further."

Cornell shrugged. "Well, it looks like I'm brainless."

Clutching his wand, Cornell trudged down the embankment, and then Cornell trudged over to the town. The town was full of deserted buildings, a great place for ghosts to haunt, he thought.

Cornell looked through several buildings, ready to vanquish them with a flick of his wand.

But Cornell saw no trace of any ghosts, not even furniture covered in old bed sheets.

So Cornell trudged back up the hill to Ty.

"Find anything?" Ty asked scornfully.

"Not yet," Cornell said. "But I won't give up until I do."

"Looks like you'll be here forever."

Ty turned on his heel and stalked back to the house.

CHAPTER TWO: WHAT CORNELL SAW IN THE FOG

They returned to the house much faster than it took them to reach the ghost town.

Rosemary had prepared dinner while they were gone. Cornell could smell the food as she opened the door.

"Professor, will you join...?"

"Yes," Cornell quickly said. "Where is the kitchen."

"This way, Professor."

The meal was simple, and Cornell helped himself to plenty of it. He ate slice after slice of dark homemade bread, spoonful after spoonful of pickled vegetables, and link after link of blood sausage.

To Cornell's surprise, Rosemary and Ty ate

very little. In fact, they only ate blood sausage, one link apiece. But this also pleased Cornell. More food for him.

The kitchen was as messy as the living room. Dirty pots and pans were stacked high everywhere, even on the table.

But Cornell didn't care because his plate and utensils had started off clean. Now that he had eaten dinner, his plate was still fairly clean, except for a few breadcrumbs and blood smears.

"Strawberry tart?" Rosemary asked, passing an old, chipped plate full of strawberry tarts.

Cornell took six. He was starting on his fourth when Rosemary asked, "Did you find any ghosts, Professor?"

"No," Cornell said, rudely speaking with his mouth full of strawberry tart. "But I will find them. Now about laundry..."

"Bring your laundry here," Rosemary instructed him. "I have an old wringer washer Ty can use."

Ty scowled.

After dessert, Cornell lumbered back to his motor home to think about this ghost problem. Ty reluctantly followed.

Cornell set his all-purpose ghost-be-gone magical wand on his aquamarine kitchen table, instead of putting it away in its case and then putting the case in the cabinet, where it belonged.

And then Cornell pointed to his dirty laundry strewn all over the motor home and heaped up in piles like mole hills.

"So?" Ty shrugged.

"I have garbage bags on the counter. You can put the laundry in there."

Ty mumbled a few bad words and then slunk off to the kitchen.

After Ty made twelve trips back and forth with all Cornell's dirty laundry, Cornell stretched across his bed to ponder the mystery.

Why would Rosemary Müller hire him to get rid of the ghosts on her lake and then not show him the lake?

And what did the ghost town have to do with the ghosts on the lake?

Cornell decided the best way to think was to sleep for a couple of hours and then do a little sleuthing in the dark. He set his alarm for midnight, a good time to look for ghosts.

BEEP! BEEP! BEEP!

Cornell fumbled for the alarm clock and switched it off. Then he fumbled around the very dark motor home for a flashlight. He finally found it under a mountain of dirty towels. Now it was Cornell's turn to scowl. He had forgotten to tell Ty to wash the towels, too.

Then Cornell picked up his picked his get-rid-of-ghosts-in-lakes briefcase and stumbled out of the motor home. Again, Cornell carefully locked the door and pocketed the key.

First stop, Cornell thought, is the lake.

But where was the lake? Cornell carefully looked around him.

Cornell did not see a lake when he drove to Rosemary's house.

Cornell did not see a lake when he walked to the ghost town with Ty.

Bur Cornell had not explored the area behind Rosemary's house. So Cornell opened his briefcase and removed his lake finder.

To most people, it looked like an old rusty harmonica, but Cornell was not most people.

Cornell rounded the side of the house, straight to the back and beyond. The lake finder picked up the spirit of the mission and started playing a tinty tune.

As Cornell walked, the air cooled and became as thick as misty pea soup. He heard the moaning of the ghosts before he actually saw them or the lake.

The lake finder played harder and louder, like a child who was blowing with all his might.

"Silence!" Cornell ordered.

The lake finder sheepishly stopped playing and slid under the cuff of Cornell's colorful patchwork blazer.

A slight breeze blew off the gray-black waters. A band of ghosts in blue coats, black boots, and tricorne hats gently swayed over the hazy waters. They moaned; they sobbed; and they looked very, very lost.

Eureka, Cornell thought. These aren't mean ghosts. They are lost and afraid ghosts.

Help us! Help us! Help us!

Cornell noticed something else. The mist covering the ghosts was only at the lake. He quickly snapped open his briefcase, grabbed his ghost banisher, and pointed it at the misty ghosts.

Nothing happened.

Help us! Help us! Help us!

Cornell scratched his black curls with his lake finder. Why were the ghosts still there?

He pointed his ghost banisher again, harder this time.

Help us! Help us! Help us!

Something is controlling them, Cornell thought. Something was controlling them and not letting them go home. That was the only reason why a ghost banisher would not work, especially this ghost banisher. Cornell was using the latest model of a DuppyGone 367, the most powerful of ghost banishers.

Cornell made up his mind.

He put his supernatural tools away, snatched his briefcase, and strode toward the motor home. He would exchange his get-rid-of-ghosts-in-lakes briefcase for his all-purpose ghost-be-gone magical wand and do some real sleuthing in the ghost town.

But with each step away from the lake, the mist grew thicker and colder. Cornell just ignored the mist. It takes more than a tiny bit of fog to deter a famous supernatural super sleuth from his mission.

The mist swirled around and around and around.

Or was it Cornell who was spinning? He stopped, spinning, and then he took an uncertain step.

His head whirled. He pressed his palm against his forehead. Why was he so dizzy?

A pair of coal black eyes stared at him.

Cornell gasped, mustered up the last of his strength, and broke into a run.

But two invisible hands shoved him down to the ground and held firmly him in place.

CHAPTER THREE: STAY AWAY FROM THE GRAVES

"What happened?" Cornell asked as he sat up and rubbed his pounding head.

He was in Rosemary's living room on a pulled-out sofa bed with moth-eaten sheets.

"You passed out in the old part of town," Rosemary said in her croaky voice. She was sitting in a chair next to the sofa bed. "Ty went looking for you when you didn't come to breakfast."

"The old part of town?" Cornell shook his head, trying to remember. "What's that?"

"The ghost town," Ty said with a sneer in his voice. "Remember? We went there yesterday."

"Right," Cornell said, although the memory was like mist, hard to see past and impossible to grasp. "Well, send breakfast to my motor home. I am going to study up on the Revolutionary War."

Rosemary and Ty looked at each other.

"You missed breakfast," Rosemary said. "And then you missed lunch. But I can make an early dinner."

Cornell snorted. "Madam, I am the great supernatural super sleuth Cornell Dyer. And I must eat three good meals a day, plus snacks, to solve the most mysterious of supernatural mysteries." Cornell swung his legs over the side of the bed. "I am going to my motor home to read up about the Revolutionary War. I expect breakfast and lunch to be served to me promptly."

Rosemary and Ty looked at each other again, longer this time.

Then Rosemary nodded.

"Very well, Professor," Rosemary croaked. "I will make the food right now. Ty will bring it out to you."

"Whatever," Ty said with a shrug.

Cornell's muscles ached, and they cramped when he tried to stand. But finally he was on his large feet and staggering to his motor home. He stumbled into the living room and over to the long bookcase, scanning the shelves.

Finally he found it – a big book about the Revolutionary War. Cornell plopped onto on his green, blue, and purple-patterned couch to read it. In fact, Cornell slouched as he read it, which was not good for his posture. However, Cornell was comfortable and did not care.

On the floor was a box of half-eaten powdered sugar doughnuts. Cornell shoved one into his mouth and turned the page.

An hour later, a very starving Cornell heard a knock on his door.

"Come in!" he called.

The door opened, and Cornell heard, "It's Ty. Grandmother made your breakfast and lunch. Do you want it on your table?"

"No. Bring it to me here."

Ty walked into the living room with a large rusty tray. Cornell pointed to the coffee table.

"Put the tray there," Cornell said.

Ty did, making a face. "Anything else?"

Cornell turned a page and. "Nope."

Ty left.

As soon as the door shut, Cornell bolted up and lifted the lid of the tray. Good. Ty had brought a lot of food. Breakfast was on the left, and lunch was on the right.

For breakfast, Rosemary had made homemade rolls with strawberry jam, sausage links, four eggs with melted cheese, thick slabs of bacon, potato pancakes, muesli, plain yogurt, and six glasses of orange juice.

For lunch, Rosemary had made four sandwiches on very dark, dense bread. The filling between the blood was odd: chopped blood sausage, crumbled cheese, and diced pickles, all held together with beet relish. On the side was a big bowl of potato salad.

Cornell munched, slurped, and turned pages. Then he saw an illustration of Hessian soldiers. They wore blue coats, black boots, and tricorne hats.

"Eureka!" Cornell cried. "The ghosts at the lake!"

Cornell kept reading.

As he read, Cornell learned that the British Army had hired thirty thousand German soldiers to help them fight during the Revolutionary War.

Cornell learned that General George Washington and the Continental Army had captured nine hundred Hessians soldiers and officers after the Battle of Trenton on December 26, 1776.

Cornell learned the soldiers were treated like kings, which wasn't bad for prisoners. But the officers had better treatment. They were sent to Virginia and set free.

Cornell stopped in mid-chew and mid-slurp.

Virginia.

Where Cornell was staying right now in a no-name town.

Where Rosemary Müller had summoned him to banish ghosts on her lake.

"'They' say part of our town was built on

buried soldiers that...died here."

But if the Hessian officers were set free, what soldiers died in Virginia? Why was the town built over them?

Cornell licked the plates and drained the last drops. Then he closed the book and stretched. Time for sleuthing!

So Cornell grabbed his all-purpose ghost-be-gone magical wand, which was still sitting on his aquamarine kitchen table where he'd tossed it after his walk with Ty.

He locked the motor home, pocketed the keys, and set out across the field. Every few minutes, Cornell swatted a mosquito or two and waved away clouds of gnats.

Finally Cornell arrived at the edge of the hill overlooking at the ghost town. But was it really a ghost town?

Cornell trudged down the embankment, and then Cornell trudged over to the town. It was full of deserted buildings, a great place for ghosts to haunt, he thought.

He looked through several buildings, ready to vanquish them with a flick of his wand. But Cornell saw no trace of any ghosts, not even furniture covered in old bed sheets.

"Hey, Sonny!" Cornell heard a gravelly voice say.

Cornell turned around. A crooked man with

a black hair, a black beard, and coal black eyes stood in front of you. He looked as dried out and wrinkled as an old raisin.

"Who are you?" Cornell asked.

"I'm Kevin Wellman," the old man said in a voice with a faint German accent. "I run the library. Who are you?"

"I am the great supernatural super sleuth Cornell Dyer. I specialize in Amulets, Fortune-Telling (with and without cards), Ghost-Hunting..."

"No! Not the great Professor Cornell Dyer! Well, this IS an honor! I have a whole shelf of books about your great abilities."

Kevin Wellman bowed low after this strange speech.

"Tell me, Professor," Kevin's coal black eyes gleamed. "Why have you come to our town?"

"I like history," Cornell said. "I'm interested in the history about the Revolutionary War."

Kevin rubbed his hands together. His eyes shone like obsidian.

"I'm especially interested in Hessians," Cornell said.

Kevin stopped smiling.

"I heard some Hessians were buried here," Cornell said. "Where are the graves?"

Kevin grabbed Cornell by his throat and hissed, "Don't go if you know what's good for you!"

Cornell tried pulling Kevin's hand off. But

Kevin just squeezed tighter.

"Anyone who goes to those graves," Kevin warned, "will be cursed forever."

Kevin let go.

Cornell panted and rubbed his neck.

Then Cornell faced Kevin and said in a firm voice, "Sir, I am the great supernatural super sleuth Cornell Dyer. I specialize in Amulets, Fortune-Telling (with and without cards), Ghost-Hunting, Horoscopes, Numerology, Palm-Reading, Potions, Séances, Spells, Vampire-Slaying, controlling zambie populations, and deactivating Moravian pink goblins and cold whispers. Now..."

Cornell took a step and looked deeply into Kevin's coal black eyes. "Are you going to tell me where to find the graves or not?"

CHAPTER FOUR: BLANK SLATE

Cornell trudged up a very steep hill on the other side of the ghost town that wasn't quite a ghost town.

Because on the other side of the ghost town was a real town, quiet, but alive. The town had a diner, a movie theater, a clothing shop, a police station, and the library, where Kevin Wellman worked.

But Cornell knew it was a real town because he saw real people in it. He didn't see many people. But every time Cornell passed a window, he saw two people, always a man with black hair and a woman with red hair.

What a strange town, Cornell thought as he walked.

But Cornell was not worried about curses.

A medicine man Cornell had met in the Canadian Rockies made sure Cornell would never worry about curses again.

Cornell had shrunk the monstrous colony of giant moose that terrorized the mountain men. In return, the medicine man had fed Cornell a big dinner of tourtière, poutine, bannock, and then he fed Cornell a gallon of freshly tapped maple syrup for dessert.

The medicine man had also given Cornell an everlasting bottle of no-stick curse solution that Cornell rubbed all over his body every Saturday night after his bath.

So Cornell was not afraid of an itsy-bitsy curse. And he wasn't afraid of big curses either. Cornell was a curse-proof as anyone could be.

When Cornell reached the top of the hill, he pulled his grave-finder out of his back pocket. The hill was so overgrown with old brown grass, the graves would be impossible to find without it.

The grave-finder buzzed whenever Cornell got close to a grave. At each grave, Cornell pulled away the thick, prickly grasses that covered the tombstone. But none of the graves had names, only dates. And the dates were the same: December 25, 1777.

Puzzled, Cornell trudged down the very tall hill and headed to the library. Kevin Wellman was helping another patron, a young woman with long red hair.

So Cornell walked up and down the aisles of the library until he came to the section about the Revolutionary War. He flipped through book after book. But Cornell found no information about the Hessians or the mysterious graves on top of the hill.

It was night when Cornell made it back to his motor home. Cornell had lots of research to do and was too tired to walk back to the house to see if Rosemary had made him dinner. And, anyway, he was too hungry to wait.

So Cornell made himself a stack of cheese sandwiches with his favorite American cheese and white bread. He sat at his aquamarine kitchen table and turned his time traveling view finder to the Revolutionary War channel.

Cornell watched every program relating to the Hessians. But he could not find out any more information.

None of the programs told Cornell what happened to the Hessian officers after they were freed in Virginia.

None of the programs explained why Hessian ghosts haunted the lake behind Rosemary Müller's house.

None of the channels even mentioned the no-name graves at the top of the hill in this no-name town.

All night, Cornell watched program after program about the Revolutionary War.

At dawn, a yawning and very sleepy Cornell decided to turn off the time traveling view finder and get some sleep.

Cornell woke up at noon, shaking and sweating, and he didn't know why. But the no-name graves on top of the hill still bothered him. He had to go back.

So Cornell ate a few bowlfuls of cold crunchy cereal and drank a giant bottle of orange juice. Then he packed a backpack full of peanut butter and jelly sandwiches from magic jars of peanut butter and jelly that spread themselves on the bread and then jumped into sandwich bags with no help from him.

Cornell also packed a couple bottles of Magic Chocolate Milk.

Magic Chocolate Milk does not need to stay in a refrigerator. Magic Chocolate Milk does not go bad, ever. Magic Chocolate Milk is the perfect drink for supernatural super sleuths when they are studying no-name Hessian graves.

The field took forever to cross. Cornell wound up eating half of his sandwiches before he ever reached the ghost town. Then it took Cornell forever to cross the ghost town and the real town and then climb the hill.

With each step, the hill grew steeper, darker, and mistier.

When he finally reached the top, it was night. Cornell was hot, tired, hungry, and sweaty.

He wiped his brow with the sleeve of his patchwork blazer. He strained to see through the thick fog. Where were the graves?

And then...

A pair of coal black eyes stared through the fog at him.

CHAPTER FIVE: NIGHTMARE?

The eyes inched closer to Cornell – and then closer and closer and closer.

Cornell turned tried to run away, but each lifting of his foot felt as if the foot were stuck in wet cement. The fog wrapped around his neck, choking him until everything turned black...

Cornell opened his eyes, shivering. He felt cold to his bones; every muscle burned like fire; and his head throbbed with foggy pain.

He tried to sit up, move an arm, or wiggle a toe, but he couldn't. Every part felt chained down, but he didn't see any chains. The ground beneath him felt moist and rocky. The misty air felt damp and smelled like old mildew and laundry soap.

A flicker like a candle flame appeared in front of him. And then a second flame lit up – and then another and another until tongues of flames danced around him, blinding him and making his skin smart from the heat.

Melted colors appeared in the flames, The colors thickened and separated until Cornell could make out their shapes.

The shapes became a band of ghosts in blue coats, black boots, and tricorne hats gently swayed in the crackling light. They moaned; they sobbed; and they looked very, very lost.

Help us! Help us! Help us!

Cornell smelled burning cloth. He smelled red-hot metal. He sweated and sweated and sweated. He felt so hot. He felt so thirsty. He felt like crayons left outside in the summer sun.

Help us! Help us! Help us!

The flames inched closer and closer. They licked his sneakers and sleeves of his colorful blazer. The figures swayed, moaned, and sobbed.

Help us! Help us! Help us!

With a roar, Cornell used all his strength to raise his head. He heard a CLANG as a sharp object hit the back of his head.

Cornell stirred at the sound of birds chirping. He jumped up and smacked his forehead into an open cabinet door. He shook his head, a little confused. Why was he sleeping on the kitchen table?

He grabbed a couple of ice cubes from the freezer and wrapped them in a dish towel. Then Cornell scurried to the bathroom and looked in the mirror.

Cornell had an angry red mark from the cabinet door that was swelling into a golf ball-sized lump.

He hurried back to the kitchen for more ice, thinking about his strange dream all the way.

CHAPTER SIX: NOT SO EMPTY AFTER ALL

Cornell lay on the coach with the ice pack on his head. He ate the rest of the powdered sugared doughnuts and tried to figure out how he got back to his motor home.

How long he was gone?

He remembered waking up at noon yesterday, shaking and sweating.

He remembered eating a few bowls of cold crunchy cereal and drinking a giant bottle of orange juice.

He remembered packing a backpack full of peanut butter and jelly sandwiches and Magic Chocolate Milk.

He'd packed the magical kind of peanut butter and jelly, the kind that spread itself on the bread and hopped into sandwich bags and then into the backpack so Cornell Dyer could concentrate on solving supernatural mysteries.

The chocolate milk was also magical because it never spoiled.

Cornell remembered it take a very long time to cross the field. He remembered it took an even longer time to find the graves.

He remembered the darkness, the mist, and the coal black eyes coming out of the mist.

But Cornell did not remember coming down the hill or walking back to his motor home or eating the rest of his peanut butter and jelly sandwiches or drinking up the Magic Chocolate Milk.

In fact, Cornell didn't see his backpack anywhere. Bur since Cornell didn't put his things away most of the time, that didn't mean it wasn't in the motor home.

But Cornell did know someone who could give him answers. He dropped the wet dish towel into the sink, ate a few bowls of cold crunchy cereal, drank another large bottle of orange juice, and then headed directly to Rosemary Müller's house.

Ty opened the door. He was not happy to see Cornell. He eyed Cornell up and down. He sniffed hard.

"I can't change my clothes," Cornell said. "You haven't brought my laundry back yet."

"I'm not done washing it," Ty retorted. "You have more laundry than a clothing store."

"I need to talk to your grandmother."

"She's busy. But you can wait in the living room while I get her."

So Cornell followed Ty into the house. Ty walked to the back of the house. Cornell went into the living room.

While Cornell waited, he took a better look around the room. He saw a lot of pictures.

Some were old black and white photographs taped onto the wall.

Some were thicky, heavy oils hanging on the walls in their thick, heavy, wooden frames.

One oil caught Cornell's attention. It was a group of Hessian soldiers.

"You need to talk to me?" a crisp, croaky voice asked.

Cornell turned around. Rosemary stood in the doorway.

"Yes," Cornell said. "You asked me to come here to get rid of ghosts. But you then you tell me I will have a hard time getting rid of them. You tell me that this no-name town was buried over soldiers. Then I find a no-name grave in a no-name town. The librarian warns me the stay away or I will be cursed forever."

"I see," Rosemary croaked in an annoyed voice. She hobbled to her rocking chair, sat, and started rocking.

Creak, creak, creak, creak, creak.

"So Professor Dyer," Rosemary croaked again. "Is this supernatural mystery too hard for you to solve?"

Cornell laughed. "Madam, I am the great supernatural super sleuth Cornell Dyer. No supernatural mystery is too hard for me to solve. In fact, I have seen your ghosts."

Creak, creak, creak, creak, creak.

"Good," Rosemary said, still rocking.

"Your Hessian ghosts," Cornell added.

Rosemary nodded, rocking.

"So my question is this," Cornell continued. "What is the strange mist at the lake and near the graves?

"Professor," Rosemary said, still rocking. "My family has lived around this town since before the Revolutionary War. Some of them fought in the war. Some had farmland. Some were merchants."

"But what about the mist?" Cornell persisted.

Creak, creak, creak, creak, creak.

"Madam?" Cornell asked.

Creak, creak, creak, creak, creak.

"Hey, Professor!" Ty called out.

Cornell turned toward the doorway. Ty was leaning against the door jamb with his arms crossed over his chest.

"Can't you see she's done talking?" Ty said.

Cornell narrowed his eyes at the disrespectful young man. Then he walked across the room and stopped right in front of Ty.

"She may be done talking," Cornell said. "But I am not done sleuthing. Your grandmother brought me here to get rid of the ghosts. And when I get here, what do I find? Another supernatural mystery! Well, the only type of supernatural mystery I like is a solved one. And solve it I will, with or without your grandmother's cooperation."

Cornell pushed past Ty and then thought of something else.

"One more thing," Cornell said. "Get my laundry done by tonight. Or else."

"Or else 'what?'" Ty asked.

Bur Cornell was already shutting the door behind him. He wasn't wasting any more time talking to Ty. He wanted to look at the ruins before it got dark. Time didn't act right here, and Cornell didn't want to be up on the hill with a new moon tonight.

Now Cornell was not afraid of the dark. And he wasn't afraid of new moons. But he did want to see where he was sleuthing. And he wanted to get a good night's sleep tonight, which was hard to do in this no-name town. He shook the thought of "sleep" out of his mind. He had a lot of work to do before bedtime.

Cornell crossed the field and reached the

ruins in no time. This was strange because it had taken him a long time to reach them last night.

He decided to take a quick walk around the outskirts to see if anything struck him as out of the ordinary.

Circling around the ghost town, Cornell estimated that fifteen, maybe twenty-five families had lived there at one time.

But where had they gone?

Did they leave town?

Or were they part of the dead under the no-name tombstones up on top of the hill?

However, Cornell could not explore anymore because it had suddenly turned quite dark. A cold chill ran up his spine, and he shuddered. Cornell wasn't afraid. But maybe it he should explore the inhabited part of town.

Cornell was hurrying in that direction when he suddenly fell backwards and felt two hands pulling him along the road.

CHAPTER SEVEN: A GRAVE INVITATION

The thing pulled Cornell, up, up, up the hill.

It pulled him past the no-name graves. It pulled him deeply into the woods.

Cornell's mind ran a mile a minute, certainly faster than the thing was pulling him. In fact, the thing pulled him very, very slowly.

What was going on, he wondered.

OUCH!

The thing had dropped Cornell onto a hard slab of rock. Cornell looked here, and Cornell looked there. Cornell looked this way and that.

The coal black eyes looked back, the same coal black eyes Cornell had seen by the lake and by the graves.

"Look deeply into my eyes," the thing said

in a soothing voice.

Now Cornell knew that when a supernatural thing gives an order like that, it's really best not to obey.

But Cornell felt too helpless not to obey. No matter how hard he tried to look somewhere else, he kept turning to look deeply into that pair of coal black eyes.

Cornell felt weak.

Then Cornell felt limp.

Finally, Cornell could not move at all.

The coal black eyes moved closer, and closer, and closer...

Cornell realized he was not in a good situation. His heart pounded. His hands trembled.

No, Cornell told himself. I refuse to be scared out of my brilliant wits. I refuse to lose to this...this thing. I am the great supernatural super sleuth Cornell Dyer.

Nothing, Cornell reminded himself absolutely nothing live, dead, or of the spirit world would get the best of him.

The eyes were so close now...he saw the outline of a skeleton dressed in black...

When Cornell woke up the next morning, he was leaning against a tree with a rolled-up note in his hand. Cornell unrolled the note and

Dear Mr. Dyer,

I have a business proposition that I want to discuss with you.

Meet me by the graves this Friday at 11:30 p.m.

Sincerely,
Kellen Wechsler

Cornell looked at the letter for a long time, trying to figure out what to do.

If the man who left him this letter was the same skeletal thing with the coal black eyes, Cornell wanted nothing to do with him.

And yet...

Cornell had a strange feel that if he didn't show up, something bad would happen to him. He tucked the letter inside a blazer pocket, stood up, and stretched. Time for breakfast!

As Cornell trudged back to town, he thought about the invitation some more.

What if that "Kellen Wechsler" was the reason for all the strange things happening in this no-name town?

But –

If Cornell met Kellen on Friday night, did that mean the no-name town could finally return to normal?

But what was normal for this town?

Could Cornell make Kellen return the town to normal? Could Cornell trust Kellen to do it, even if he made Kellen do it?

Or would Cornell simply figure out how to subdue Kellen to reset the town?

If Cornell met Kellen, would the ghosts go away? Or would the job still fall to Cornell?

Still...

Kellen and the ghosts were connected in some way. Cornell was certain of it.

But how?

Cornell stopped to catch his breath. Yes, he was out of shape, and he had done a lot of walking lately.

But his mind was swarming with many, many thoughts. It made Cornell dizzy, like he might pass out. He stopped and braced himself against a tree, panting.

"I am the great supernatural super sleuth Cornell Dyer," Cornell said aloud. "I specialize in Amulets, Fortune-Telling (with and without cards), Ghost-Hunting, Horoscopes, Numerology, Palm-Reading, Potions, Séances, Spells, Vampire-Slaying, controlling zambie populations, and deactivating Moravian pink goblins and cold whispers. I WILL solve the mystery of Hessian ghosts and mysterious mists with coal black eyes that look like skeletons and leave notes in the night. All I need is a good breakfast.

And with that, Cornell let go of the tree and continued with his journey into town.

CHAPTER EIGHT: REDHEAD – AND DEAD

When Cornell reached the real town on the other side of the ghost town, he headed straight for the diner.

Yes, Cornell had food in his motor home.

Yes, Cornell knew Rosemary was supposed to cook for him.

But Cornell was hungry now. He didn't have time to make his own food or wait for Rosemary to cook some for him.

So Cornell went into the diner. The diner's décor was black and white with hints of red here and there.

Like the cushioned stops of the stools at the counter and the cushioned tops of the chairs and the benches at the booths.

Like the coffee cups.

And like the waitress's hair.

The diner only had one other person inside right now. And he was dressed in black from head to toe. He was sitting in a booth in the way back, drinking a cup of coffee.

And this customer had coal black eyes, just like the eyes Cornell kept seeing in the mist.

Cornell felt like screaming.

But Cornell also felt like eating.

Cornell reminded himself that supernatural super sleuths don't scream. They eat and solve supernatural mysteries.

Who knows? Maybe this customer was part of the mystery.

Maybe Cornell would solve the mystery if he ate at this diner.

So Cornell tiptoed to the other end of the diner, hoping the man in black would not see him.

Then Cornell quietly slipped into a booth and opened the menu. The menu had only one item: the daily special.

The special consisted of homemade rolls with strawberry jam, sausage links, four eggs with melted cheese, thick slabs of bacon, potato pancakes, muesli, plain yogurt, and six glasses of orange juice.

"Waddya have?" the read-headed waitress with the green eyes asked, holding her pencil above her order pad.

"I'll have the special," Cornell said.

She scrawled that across the page. "Comin' right up."

The food arrived almost immediately. Cornell ate bite after bite, thinking that the food tasted very familiar. Where had he eaten food like this? He could not remember.

Oh, well, Cornell thought as he gulped down a glass of orange juice. Who cares?

Just as Cornell stuffed the last strip of bacon into his mouth, he felt a cold, cold chill run up his spine.

Cornell turned his head slightly. The man was staring at him with his coal black eyes.

You had better show up Friday night, the man said in a faint German accent without moving his lips. *Or you will dearly regret it.*

Cornell slumped deeply into his chair. He'd had a lot of crazy dreams since he'd come to this no-name town. Was this one of them?

He closed his eyes, hoping to wake up in his motor home. Instead, he felt a shake on his shoulder.

Cornell opened his eyes. The waitress was staring down at him.

"Coffee?" she asked.

Cornell nodded it.

"You look pale," she said and quickly filled his cup. "You OK, mister?"

Cornell sat up, nodded, and took a big gulp of coffee.

And he wondered if he could disappear before Friday night.

Now Cornell had never run away from a supernatural mystery. But he had never encountered one that kept outsmarting him.

What did that man mean, that I would regret now showing up, Cornell wondered again?

Cornell finished his coffee, paid his bill, and left the diner. He kept thinking about the mystery as he tripped across the field, back to his motor home, and all the way to his bed, where he collapsed into a fitful sleep.

In his dreams, Cornell kept showing up at the graveyard on the hill. The stranger with the coal black eyes kept weaving in and out of each dream frame.

With a start, Cornell woke up. He was covered in sweat, and his bedroom was hot and bright. He grabbed his alarm clock. Three o'clock!

Cornell struggled to get up and then struggled to walk to the kitchen for a drink of water. His head pounded as he sipped. What was happening to him?

A hard rap on the door stopped hurt his head and stopped his thoughts.

Cornell set the glass down and opened the door. A police officer with black hair and dark sunglasses was standing there. His badge read Keegan O'Wiley.

"Top 'o' the afternoon to ye," the police

officer said with a faint German accent. "I'm here to ask ye some questions about Rhoda Mason."

"Rhoda Mason?" Cornell repeated. "I don't know anyone called Rhoda Mason."

"Sure ye do," the police officer said with a grin. "She's a waitress at the no-name diner. Folks say you're the last one to see her alive."

"Huh? The waitress? She's dead?"

"Her body was found by the ruins." The police officer grinned. "Hear you've been down at the ruins o'lot lately."

"This is true," Cornell said. "But I am here to solve a mystery, not create one. You might want to question the other man at the diner."

"Other man?"

"Yes. The man with the coal black eyes. He was already there when I arrived for breakfast."

The officer made a note of that and then tipped his hat.

"Thank ye for your help, sir," he said. "I will go check it out."

After the officer left, Cornell shut the door and sank to the floor.

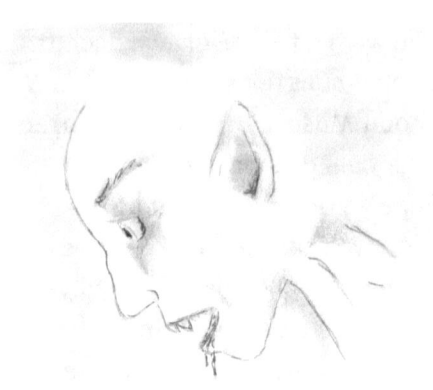

CHAPTER NINE: HE DOESNT ACT
LIKE A VAMPIRE

Cornell did not sit on the floor for long. Shortly after the officer left, Cornell snapped back to attention.

The man with the coal black eyes must have killed the red-headed waitress. No one else in this town dared to go anywhere near the ruins.

So what kind of person...thing...was this being?

What would happen to Cornell if he didn't meet with him on Friday night?

What would happen to Cornell if he did?

First up: lunch.

Second up: research on mistical beings.

Cornell opened several cans of spaghetti and dumped them into a big mixing bowl without even taking the time to heat the spaghetti up.

Then Cornell grabbed a big spoon and a bottle of his favorite orange drink. He carried them into his living room and set them on the coffee table.

Cornell took off the dusty plastic dust cover to his phonograph, knocking a group of sleeping goblins to the floor in the process.

"Hey, buddy!" they grumbled, swiping at the seat of their pants and glaring at him. "Watch what you're doing!"

Cornell selected his favorite Wagnerian opera from his record collection. As he pulled the record out of its sleeve, Cornell's missing recipe for turning princes back into frogs fell out. But Cornell was too busy to pick up the recipe now. Cornell had a supernatural mystery to solve. He'd have Ty pick it up later.

Then Cornell scanned his bookshelves for a book on mistical beings. Cornell had lots of books. But he didn't keep them in any particular order. And he had stacked books in front of other books and on top of other books.

This system made it hard for him to find what he wanted when he wanted it.

A miniature unicorn landed on his shoulder and pointed to three books with its rainbow horn.

"Why these three?" Cornell asked.

The unicorn shrugged, and sprinkles flew into the air and landed onto the rug, next to the other sprinkles Cornell hadn't vacuumed. But that was OK. He'd have Ty clean it up later.

Instead, Cornell settled onto the couch to eat spaghetti, listen to opera, and read up on mistical beings.

And, yes, he put his feet up on the coffee table without even taking off his oversized sneakers, which is rude and scuffs the table.

Cornell skimmed the pages until he came to a part that made him sit up in surprise.

Vampires are experts at shapeshifting. They can disguise themselves in a variety of ways, the most common ones being that of a wolf or a dog, a bat and fog or mist.

Mist? Was that thing with the coal black eyes a vampire? Cornell felt his neck. No bite marks. If this thing were a vampire, why hadn't it bit Cornell's neck?

Cornell kept reading and learned lots of new information about vampires.

Vampires have the traits of humans, but they're more dead-looking.

Older vampires can come out into the sunlight only for short periods of time.

Older vampires can eat human food, but the food might come back up later.

Vampires have sharp teeth that only appear when feeding.

Vampires don't just bite necks. They can take blood from cheeks, thighs, fingers, toes, or below the heart.

Vampires can put a person under their control.

Vampires have great strength and can teleport into other eras and locations.

Vampires must carry some earth from where it came.

There are only two known ways to kill a vampire. Hammer an oak stake through its heart to sever its head with a silver dagger.

All this vampire knowledge was interesting. But it wasn't helping Cornell with his current supernatural mystery.

Cornell thought and thought, and the gears cranked inside his head.

He thought: I this thing is a vampire, and if this thing wanted to kill me, it would have killed me already.

So Cornell decided the vampire must want something else.

But what?

Cornell also had another problem: time.

Ordinarily, Cornell didn't care about time. But now he was counting every day, every hour, every minute, and every second until Friday night.

And it was now Friday night. And Cornell now cared about time.

But before Cornell met with Kellen, he stopped at Rosemary's house and told her that he was very close to solving the mystery.

"I'm so happy to hear it," Rosemary croaked as she rocked. "After all these years, we will finally rest in peace."

A few minutes later, Cornell was trotting across the field to the ruins. He reached the ghost town at ten o'clock by his ElStation Rodic 73 watch.

Without stopping, Cornell hurried through the ghost town, the actual town that now looked like a ghost town (which added to the mystery) and up the hill.

An hour later, Cornell was passing the cemetery with the no-name headstones and into the deep part of the woods. The farther Cornell walked, the foggier and mistier it grew. Cornell knew he was early, but he was afraid of the consequences if he were late.

As Cornell paused to catch his breath, he heard a faintly German voice say, "Mr. Dyer, you're early."

CHAPTER TEN: I HAVE A JOB FOR YOU

Out of the grayish gloom, a cloaked figure appeared. It was dressed in black from head to toe.

Its hair was black.

Its eyes were coal black.

Its lips were very red.

It was Kellen Wechsler.

Cornell took a deep breath and said, "That's 'Professor' to you."

"Of course," Kellen said. "'Professor.'"

"What do you want me with?" Cornell asked in the calmest voice he could muster.

Kellen smiled. "There's no need to be afraid, Professor Dyer." He took a step forward. "I know you know what I am. And I know you know what I can do to you."

Cornell took several steps back and bumped into a tree. "So if you're not here to kill me, what do you want?"

"I have a job for you," Kellen said. "I have a job for the great supernatural super sleuth Cornell Dyer."

"What's the job?"

"I want you to slay a vampire for me."

"That's it?"

Kellen nodded. "I have no training in slaying vampires."

"Why do you want me to slay a vampire like...like you?"

"He is not like me!!!""

Cornell jumped and hit his head again. "OK, fine. He's not like you. But why do you want me to slay him?"

"Because." Kellen frowned. "Because he became a vampire by accident."

"By accident?"

"He was a man that belonged to me. And he is trying to become a man again."

"I don't kill people."

"I don't want you to kill a person!!!"

Cornell was smart enough not to jump again. Instead, he swallowed hard and said, "Mr. Wechsler, I don't understand."

"You don't need to understand. You just need to sign this."

Kellen snapped his fingers. A scroll and a

red pen appeared. Kellen shook out the scroll and ten feet of paper unrolled from it.

He held out the pen to Cornell. "Just sign at the bottom."

"Why?" Cornell asked suspiciously. "What am I signing?"

"Just my contract," Kellen said silkily. "It says you will slay the vampire when I summon you. And any other vampires that get in my way."

"I don't slay vampires for free."

Kellen reached into his pocket and pulled out a bag. He jiggled it, and Cornell heard jingles.

"Do you hear that?" Kellen said. "A bag full of gold coins from medieval Germany. Your sign-on bonus – once you sign on."

As if in a dream, Cornell took the pen from Kellen and signed his name with red ink. Then he gave the pen back to Kellen. And then Kellen handed him the bag.

"So where is this vampire?" Cornell asked.

"I'll let you know," Kellen said. "When I'm ready, I'll let you know."

Kellen bowed and started to fade into the mist and then quickly reappeared.

"Oh, by the way," Kellen said with a gleam in his coal black eyes. "You may tell Rosemary Müller that her ghost problem is fixed."

Cornell pointed his finger at Kellen, from the hand not holding the bag of gold.

"You!" Cornell exclaimed. "It was you

controlling them all along."

Kellen rubbed his hands together. "But of course."

"Why?"

"Why?" Kellen mimicked. "Why? Why, to lure you here, of course. Haven't you ever heard of bait?"

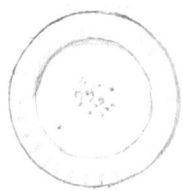

EPILOGUE

The next morning, Cornell headed over to Rosemary's house to eat breakfast with Rosemary and Ty.

Cornell also wanted to let Rosemary know that the ghosts were gone, that he expected to be paid promptly, and that Ty needed to put all of Cornell's clean laundry away.

"Hang my jeans in the closet," Cornell instructed him as he bit into a homemade roll with strawberry jam.

Ty scowled as he picked up a large garbage bag full of Cornell's clean clothes.

"Hang my T-shirts in the closet, too," Cornell said as he shoved an entire sausage link into his mouth.

"And your socks?" Ty asked sarcastically

as Cornell jammed an entire egg topped with melted cheese into his mouth.

"Last two dresser drawers," Cornell said, reaching for the last strip of bacon.

Cornell finished off the potato pancakes, muesli, yogurt, and the last of the orange juice.

Rosemary counted out his pay in medieval gold coins.

"What's with all the medieval gold coins?" Cornell asked, somewhat irritably. "Everybody wants to pay me in medieval gold coins all of a sudden."

"Got something against gold coins?" Ty retorted.

Cornell looked up and saw the ire in Ty's coal black eyes. Then he looked at the glint in Rosemary's green eyes.

"Not at all," Cornell said hastily as he bagged up the coins. "I'm just in a hurry. I have another supernatural mystery to solve."

Cornell hurried out of the house and into the motor home, happy to get away. He hoped that he would never...

BEEP! BEEP! BEEP!

Cornell fumbled for his alarm clock at the same time the phone under his pillow started ringing.

As Cornell silenced the alarm, he knocked a paper plate to the floor, scattering the crumbs of the last Turkey Delight from Mrs. Beaver.

"Is this the world famous supernatural super sleuth Cornell Dyer?" the panicked voice on the other end asked.

"Sure," Cornell mumbled sleepily.

"Do you specialize in Amulets, Fortune-Telling (with and without cards), Ghost-Hunting, Horoscopes, Numerology, Palm-Reading, Potions, Séances, Spells, Vampire-Slaying, controlling zambie populations, and deactivating Moravian pink goblins and cold whispers?"

"Sure."

"Great! I need a substitute teacher. Please come right away!"

THE FACTS IN THE FICTION

The British Army really did hire thirty thousand German soldiers to help fight on their side during the Revolutionary War.

General George Washington and the Continental Army really did capture about nine thousand soldiers after the Battle of Trenton on December 26, 1776.

The soldiers were treated very well. The officers were taken to Virginia and freed.

These German soldiers were called Hessians because many (but not all) came from the German state of Hesse-Cassel.

Many people know vampires bite the necks of people and drink their blood.

But many different countries and cultures have their own vampire legends, too. Some of the other legends are included in Cornell Dyer's research and in other books in the BryonySeries.

The food that Rosemary Müller prepares for Cornell is actual German cuisine.

The food that Cornell ate in Canada is part of the cuisine of certain regions in Canada.

About the Author

Denise M. Baran-Unland is the author of the BryonySeries supernatural/literary trilogy for young and new adults, the Adventures of Cornell Dyer chapter book series for grade school children and the Bertrand the Mouse series for young children.

She has six adult children, three adult step-children, fourteen total grandchildren, six godchildren, and four cats.

She is the co-founder of WriteOn Joliet and previously taught features writing for a homeschool coop, with the students' work published in the co-op magazine and The Herald-News in Joliet.

Denise blogs daily and is currently the features editor at The Herald-News. To read her feature stories, visit theherald-news.com. For more information about Denise's fiction and to follow her on social media, visit bryonyseries.com.

Sue Midlock lives in Illinois with her husband and has been writing for 10 years. She started writing when the book "Twilight" first came out and fell in love with the paranormal genre.

Since then, she has written and finished her Rosewood Trilogy and just recently her anniversary edition, "Forever," which is the first book re-written for adults.

Her most recent releases are "Southern Shorts," which is an anthology of short stories about Dry Prong, Louisana and "Night Games

Rebekah Baran has a knack in learning tech-nology very quickly and easily taught herself the basics of website design, formatting manuscripts for print books and eBooks, book cover design, and the basics of self-publishing.

Baran earned an Associate of Applied Science in Culinary Arts from Joliet Junior College in 2016 and has worked as a pastry chef, prep cook, and assistant sous chef in Will County restaurants.

She loves, baking, cooking, reading, researching new products, and all things pertaining to Asian culture.

Contact Baran at purpleroses33@gmail.com